For information address Disney • Lucasfilm Press,
1101 Flower Street, Glendale, California 91201.

Printed in China
First Hardcover Edition, July 2016   10 9 8 7 6 5 4 3 2 1

ISBN 978-1-4847-8669-7
FAC-023680-16195

Visit the official *Star Wars* website at: www.starwars.com
This book was printed on paper created from a sustainable source.

STAR WARS

Size Matters Not

Los Angeles • New York

Book Six

The battle of Hoth had barely finished raging. Darth Vader had discovered the rebel base on the frozen planet and sent his forces to attack it, leaving the rebels no choice but to flee. Rebel pilots had kept the attackers busy outside the base, allowing Han Solo to leave on the *Millennium Falcon* with Chewbacca, C-3PO, and Princess Leia.

Dodging laser blasts, Han piloted the *Falcon* away from Hoth and the destruction caused by the Empire.

Meanwhile, in another sector of space, Luke Skywalker set his course for the Dagobah system. His old Jedi Master, Obi-Wan Kenobi, had instructed him to go there to find and train with another Jedi Master, Yoda.

Luke wanted to be a Jedi Knight more than anything. Obi-Wan had taught him about the Force and about using his lightsaber. But then Darth Vader had struck Obi-Wan down. Luke knew he needed a Jedi Master who could complete his training.

He had to find Yoda.

Dagobah was covered in a layer of fog, and the ground was impossible to see. As Luke tried to land, he lost control of his X-wing. The ship splashed down in a swamp, sinking half underwater.

"You stay put," Luke told R2-D2. "I'll have a look around."

Luke made sure the area was safe, then set up camp. Still, he thought there was something strange about the place. "I feel like—" he started to say.

Suddenly, he heard a noise behind him. Luke whirled around, drawing his blaster.

"Like we're being watched," Luke finished, spotting a small, wrinkly creature with huge ears and green skin.

"Away put your weapon!" the creature said. "I mean you no harm. Help you, I can."

Luke doubted very much that the strange little creature could help him. He seemed like he could barely help himself. But what harm was there in asking for help? "I'm looking for a Jedi Master," he explained.

"You seek Yoda," the creature replied with a sly smile. The creature promised to take Luke to Yoda. But first he brought Luke to a small mud hut.

Luke was getting impatient. The little green creature still hadn't told him when he would meet Yoda.

"Will it take us long to get there?" Luke asked.

"Yoda not far," the creature said. He puttered around, making dinner.

But Luke wanted to see Yoda right away.

"We're wasting our time!" he cried.

The creature sighed. "I cannot teach him," he said quietly. "The boy has no patience."

"He will learn patience," someone replied. It was Obi-Wan Kenobi's voice! Luke was shocked to hear the spirit of his old mentor.

"Much anger in him, like his father," the creature said, shaking his head. "He is not ready."

Suddenly, Luke understood. The small green creature *was* Yoda! And Yoda didn't seem impressed with him.

"Adventure," Yoda said. "Excitement. Ha! A Jedi craves not these things."

"I won't fail you," Luke said. Yoda *had* to train him. "I'm not afraid!"

"Oh, you will be," Yoda said. He looked very stern. "You will be."

Luke threw himself into his training with Yoda. Every day he got a little better. But the training took everything he had. Luke had never been so tired in his entire life.

"A Jedi's strength flows from the Force," Yoda told him. "But beware the dark side. Consume you it will, as it did Obi-Wan's apprentice."

"Vader," Luke said. He knew that Darth Vader had once been a Jedi, before he went to the dark side.

One day, Luke and Yoda walked to a cave in the swamp. The dark side was strong here.

Yoda sent Luke in armed with only his lightsaber. Inside, the young Jedi found Darth Vader waiting for him. Luke battled and defeated him, but when he removed Vader's mask, he saw his own face.

The duel had been a test.

And Luke had failed. He had attacked Vader with fear and anger rather than trusting in the Force.

Luke continued his training. He learned to use the Force to lift things into the air. At first it was small things, like sticks and stones. But soon Luke was able to levitate larger rocks . . . while standing on one hand . . . with Yoda balanced on his foot! Luke felt pretty proud of himself!

Then Yoda told Luke to use the Force to raise his sinking ship.

"All right," Luke said. "I'll give it a try."

"No!" Yoda said. "Do. Or do not. There is no try."

Luke reached out with the Force, straining to lift the ship. The craft rose a few inches out of the murky water. But Luke lost focus, and the ship sank completely.

"Size matters not," Yoda said. Closing his eyes, the Jedi Master extended his hand. Luke watched in amazement as his X-wing began to rise out of the swamp. Soon the ship was back on dry ground.

"I don't believe it!" Luke said.

"*That* is why you fail," Yoda replied.

Luke was now more determined than ever to complete his training. Then, one day, the Force showed him a vision of Han Solo and Princess Leia. They were in trouble! They had been captured by Darth Vader.

"It is the future you see," Yoda explained when Luke told him about the mysterious vision.

"I've got to go to them!" Luke cried.

Yoda tried to stop Luke from leaving. He knew he was still vulnerable to the dark side. But Luke refused to listen. He had to save his friends!

Suddenly, a glowing image of Obi-Wan appeared beside Yoda. "This is a dangerous time for you," Obi-Wan said to Luke, "when you will be tempted by the dark side of the Force."

Luke had failed his test in the cave. Yoda and Obi-Wan feared he would fail against the real Vader, too.

Still Luke would not listen. He grabbed his lightsaber and went to his ship, where R2-D2 was already waiting for him.

"Told you, I did," Yoda told Obi-Wan as Luke flew away. "Reckless is he."

"That boy is our last hope," Obi-Wan said. The fate of the entire galaxy rested on the shoulders of Luke Skywalker.

But Yoda knew Luke was not alone. "No," he corrected Obi-Wan. "There is another." And the Force would be with them both.